An I Can Read Chapter Book™

Billy the Ghost and Me

CACTUS JUNCTION

story by **Gery Greer** and **Bob Ruddick**
pictures by **Roger Roth**

HarperCollins*Publishers*

To our niece, Erin
—G.G. & B.R.

To my niece,
Alyssa Harley Friedman
—R.R.

HarperCollins®, 💾®, and I Can Read Book®
are trademarks of HarperCollins Publishers Inc.

Billy the Ghost and Me
Text copyright © 1997 by Gery Greer and Bob Ruddick
Illustrations copyright © 1997 by Roger Roth
Printed in the U.S.A. All rights reserved.

Library of Congress Cataloging-in-Publication Data
Greer, Gery.
  Billy the Ghost and me / story by Gery Greer and Bob Ruddick ; pictures by
Roger Roth.
      p.   cm. — (An I can read book)
  Summary: Young Sarah, with the help of her friend Billy the Ghost, proves
herself as a deputy by planning the perfect capture of two bank robbers in her
Western town of Cactus Junction.
  ISBN 0-06-026782-8 — ISBN 0-06-026783-6 (lib. bdg.)
  ISBN 0-06-444214-4 (pbk.)
  [1. Cowgirls—Fiction.   2. Ghosts—Fiction.   3. Robbers and outlaws—
Fiction.   4. West (U.S.)—Fiction.]   I. Ruddick, Bob.   II. Roth, Roger, ill.
III. Title.   IV. Series.
PZ7.G85347Bi   1997   95-35723
[Fic]—dc20   CIP
                                                                          AC

1   2   3   4   5   6   7   8   9   10
❖
First Edition

Contents

1. The Bank Robbery   5

2. Spiders!   15

3. Stagecoach Getaway   22

4. All Tied Up   35

5. A Silver Star   43

Chapter 1
The Bank Robbery

My name is Sarah. I live in Cactus Junction. And I know a ghost.

I am the only one who can see or hear him. Don't ask me why. I guess I'm just stuck with him.

Billy the Ghost is his name, and he is a big pain! He is always making trouble.

Last Saturday morning I was out in front of Higbee's General Store, practicing with my lasso. I looked up and saw Billy on the roof. He had a big grin on his face and an egg in his hand. He was about to drop the egg on Mrs. Purdy's head!

"Billy!" I yelled.
"Don't you dare
drop that egg!"
"Oops!" said Billy.
He hid the egg behind
his back.
"Sarah," said Mrs. Purdy,
"who are you talking to?"
"Uh, nobody," I said.
"I see," she said,
and hurried away.

Billy floated down from the roof.

"Hand over that egg," I said.

"Egg? What egg?" he asked.

"The one behind your back," I said.

"Oh, *this* egg," he said. "I was about to eat it for breakfast."

"Billy," I said, "you are a ghost. You don't eat."

"Good point," he said. "Would you care for an egg?"

Suddenly, we heard a shout. "HELP!
THE BANK HAS BEEN ROBBED!"

It was Mr. Beamer, the owner of the bank.

"Two men got away with all the
money!" he yelled.

"Let's get after them," said Sheriff Botts. "I need some deputies to help catch the robbers."

This was my chance. I have always wanted to be a deputy. "I am ready," I said.

"You are too young," said Sheriff Botts.

"I can ride and I can rope," I said.

"And you can stay at home where you belong," he said.

Everyone laughed—except for me.

Most of the men joined the sheriff. They jumped on their horses and rode out of town in a cloud of dust.

I saw something through the cloud.

I saw two women.

I saw two very strange women.

They had big muscles and hairy arms.

They wore boots, and one of them had a

mustache!

"Wow, are those ladies ugly!" said Billy.

"Look again," I said. "Those are not ladies."

"Hey, those are guys," he said. "Wow, are they ugly!"

"Look at that sack," I said. "They must be the robbers. We can't let them get away!"

"I could throw my egg at them," said Billy.

"No," I said. "Let's follow them."

I couldn't believe my eyes. The robbers went into Sheriff Botts's office!

The contestants gathered at the starting line with Team Dynamic Dragicorn on one side and Sparkle Pop and Ella on the other. Glitter Star pulled the last slug off his body. Owen patted the slug that was stuck to the top of his snout. "That's for good luck, Grossy." The stinky slug squeaked back at Owen.

"Ready . . . set . . . GO!" Ella yelled.

The four contestants rocketed off the starting line. Sparkle Pop, Glitter Star, and Ella jumped over the Rotten Swamp Log with ease. Grossy, the slug on Owen's snout, slid back on top of his eyes. Owen couldn't see and tripped over the log, tumbling head over claws, before steadying himself back to his feet.

Chapter 2
Spiders!

Billy and I hid outside.

"Haw, haw!" said the robber with the mustache. "Nobody's here. Everyone is out looking for us."

"Let's sit in the sheriff's chair!" said the other robber. "I have always wanted to sit in a sheriff's chair."

"Hey, this chair spins."

"I have a plan," I whispered to Billy.

"I'll go around to the side window," I said. "Then I'll toss these coins into the jail cell. The robbers will go in to see what made the noise. Then you slam the cell door shut."

"Good thinking," said Billy.

"Give me a twirl," said the robber sitting in the sheriff's chair. "I want to see how fast I can go."

"No fair," said the other robber. "It's my turn."

"Oh, yeah? Says who?"

I was just about to drop the coins. Then I saw Billy. Oh, no! He had a bunch of fake spiders in his hand and a big grin on his face.

Billy dropped the spiders on the robbers' heads.

"YEOW!" they yelled, and leaped into the air. They raced around the office and ran out the door.

"Billy!" I yelled. "You ruined our plan!"

"Sorry, Sarah," he said. "I didn't know they would run away. I was just having some fun."

"This is no time to fool around," I said. "This is serious. Come on, let's go after them!"

We ran down the street. The bank robbers were climbing into a stagecoach.

"They are going to escape. We have to stop them!" I said. "I have an idea."

I told Billy about it as we ran over to the stage. Billy floated up to the driver's seat, and I climbed inside.

My heart was pounding, but I put on a
sunny smile.

"Howdy, ladies," I said.

Chapter 3
Stagecoach Getaway

"Well, well!" said one of the robbers. "What a cute little girl. Isn't she cute, Mabel?"

"Cute as a button, Doris," said the other.

I heard Billy snap the reins. I leaned out the window and looked back. The driver was running after us.

"Hey, look," I said. "There's Hank, the stagecoach driver."

The robbers leaned out the window.

Quickly I untied their shoes.

"So that's the driver," said the robber named Doris. "Nice-looking fellow. A good runner, too."

"Look, he is waving to us," said Mabel.

The robbers waved back.

"Toodle-oo!" they called.

"Wait a minute . . ." said Doris.

"If that's the driver . . ." said Mabel.

"THEN WHO IS DRIVING THE STAGECOACH?" they yelled together.

They looked up at the driver's seat.

I knew they couldn't see Billy. Only I can see Billy. While they were busy, I moved fast. I started to tie Doris's shoelace to Mabel's shoelace.

"THERE IS NOBODY DRIVING THIS THING!" cried Mabel.

"WE ARE GONERS!" yelled Doris.

I didn't have time to finish.

The robbers fell back into their seats.

Their faces were as white as paper.

"Oh, didn't you know?" I said. "There is no driver on this stagecoach. These are trained horses. Hank just tells them where to go. Then they go there by themselves."

"Those are smart horses!" said Mabel.

"Let's steal them!" said Doris.

Mabel jabbed him with his elbow. "You mean *buy* them, Doris."

"Oh, right. Of course, Mabel. Heh, heh. *Buy* them."

I was thinking about their shoelaces. What was I going to do? I hadn't finished tying them together!

I could feel the stagecoach turning. That was part of the plan. Billy was heading back toward town.

The robbers were busy peeking into the
money sack.

"Good heavens, Mabel!" cried Doris.
"Will you look at this?"

"I'm looking, Doris. I'm looking!" cried Mabel.

The robbers saw me watching them. They smiled big sweet smiles.

"This is a sack of, uh, potatoes," said Mabel. "Doris and I did some shopping in Cactus Junction. Didn't we, Doris?"

"Mercy me, we sure did, Mabel! We love potatoes!"

"How many potatoes do you think we have, Doris, dear?"

"Maybe five thousand, Mabel! Maybe more!"

"Glory be! Hand them over, Doris. I want to hold them."

"Mabel, dearest, take your grubby hands off the sack."

"Oh, Doris. How you do talk. Do you want me to give you a bloody nose?"

"You and who else, Mabel, dear?"

Suddenly I heard Billy shout from above. "HEY, SARAH!"

Of course the robbers couldn't hear him. Only I can hear him.

"WE WILL BE BACK IN TOWN SOON," he called.

"I think I'll go up on top," I said to the robbers. "I want to watch the horses."

"Fine," said Doris. "Mabel and I will stay here. We have to count our potatoes."

"That's right," said Mabel. "Now let go of that sack, Doris, dear, if you want to keep all your teeth."

I climbed out the window and pulled myself up on top of the stagecoach.

Chapter 4
All Tied Up

"I didn't tie Mabel's shoelace to Doris's shoelace," I whispered to Billy. "I didn't have time."

"Let me try," Billy said.

"Okay," I said. "I will keep them busy."

"Hey, ladies!" I shouted. "Look over to the left! That is the famous, uh . . . Duck Rock. It looks like a duck."

"Wow! It *does* look like a duck!" cried Doris.

"Will you get your fat head out of the window, Doris, dear?" said Mabel. "I can't see the duck."

"Now, be polite, Mabel. Or I will have to teach you some manners. *Oof!*"

"Move over, Doris, dearest. Unless you would like to be a dead duck."

"Oh, yeah? *Ouch!* Hey, no pinching!"

Billy floated up next to me.

"All done!" he said with a grin. "I am the ghost with the most!"

"Good job," I said, and smiled.

We passed a sign. It said:

CACTUS JUNCTION, ONE MILE.

"Look," we heard Doris say. "We are coming into Cactus Junction."

"Sounds like a nice town," said Mabel.

"Sounds familiar, too," said Doris.

"Wait a minute . . ." said Mabel.

"Cactus Junction?" said Doris.

"THAT'S WHERE WE ROBBED THE BANK!" they yelled.

Doris tried to climb out of the right
window. Mabel tried to climb out of the
left window. But they couldn't get far,
because their shoelaces were tied together.

"TURN THIS STAGECOACH
AROUND!" they yelled.

I was ready with my lasso. First I lassoed Doris's hand. Then I lassoed Mabel's hand and tied their hands together across the top of the stagecoach. They could hardly move.

Suddenly the stagecoach hit a bump. I was thrown close to Mabel. He reached out with his free hand and grabbed my arm!

"All right, little girl," Mabel growled. "Now untie us and turn this stagecoach around . . . or else!"

Chapter 5
A Silver Star

I reached behind me. "Billy!" I yelled. "A spider, quick!"

Billy put a huge fake spider in my hand.

I held it in front of Mabel's face.

"When this spider bites, it kills in five seconds flat," I said.

I put the spider on his nose.

Mabel screamed and let go of my arm.

I scrambled out of reach.

"Fast thinking, Sarah," Billy said.

I grinned at him. "We make a pretty good team, don't we?" I said.

"The best," he said.

The stagecoach raced into town. We pulled up in front of the sheriff's office.

Sheriff Botts and the men were back.

"Meet Mabel and Doris," I called out. "The bank robbers."

Everyone looked at me. They looked at the robbers. Then they all cheered.

Sheriff Botts put the robbers in jail.

"Good job, Sarah!" he said. "You are my number one deputy!"

He pinned a silver star on me.

"I had help," I said, "from a ghost named Billy."

Sheriff Botts laughed. "Then your ghost can be a deputy, too," he said.

Sheriff Botts didn't believe me, but I didn't mind. Billy and I were deputies!

I looked around for Billy. He was busy
tying tin cans to the back of the stagecoach.

"Billy!" I whispered. "You can't do that!
You are a deputy now."

"Me?" said Billy. "A deputy?"

"Yes, you," I said. "So shape up."

"Maybe I should go get my egg," said
Billy. "I put it on the sheriff's chair."

"What?" I cried. "You put it where?"

Just then we heard a yell from inside the sheriff's office. "What in tarnation? Yuck! IT'S ALL OVER MY PANTS!"

"Billy!" I cried.

"Oops!" said Billy. "Maybe I had better go get the spider I put in the sheriff's desk drawer. What do you think?"

"I think you are a big pain," I said.

But I couldn't help smiling when I said it.